To Mom, Dad, Greg, Sue, and my Six Siblings

E
292-8342

©1999 by Linda Martin.
All rights reserved.
Book design by Jane Coats.
Typeset in Stempel Garamond.
The illustrations in this book were rendered in watercolors, acrylic and pen & ink.
Printed in Hong Kong.

Library of Congress Cataloging-in-Publication Data
Martin, Linda, 1961-
   When dinosaurs go to school / by Linda Martin.
   p. cm.
Summary: Dinosaurs spend a day at school with reading, writing, arithmetic, music, fingerpaints, exercise, and pizza.
ISBN 0-8118-2089-0
[1. Dinosaurs—Fiction. 2. Schools—Fiction. 3. Stories in rhyme.]
I. Title.
PZ8.3.M41216Wf 1999
[E]—dc2   98-34160   CIP
                              AC

Distributed in Canada by Raincoast Books
8680 Cambie Street, Vancouver, British Columbia V6P 6M9

10 9 8 7 6 5 4 3 2 1

Chronicle Books
85 Second Street,
San Francisco, California 94105

www.chroniclebooks.com

When Dinosaurs Go to School

Linda Martin

chronicle books·san francisco

When dinosaurs go off to school,
they like to look their best.
They wash behind their ears and scales,
and they're always nicely dressed.

They have a healthy breakfast,
and eat a piece of fruit.
They give their Mom and Dad a hug,
and out the door they scoot.

Here comes the yellow school bus.
They find a seat inside.
They laugh and talk
and make new friends.
It's a very happy ride.

At last they reach the schoolhouse,
where some have come by car.

And some have even walked to school,
for they don't live very far.

The school bell rings to start the day.
How bright the classroom looks!
They start with spelling lessons,
then read their storybooks.

Next they paint with fingerpaints.
They're squishy, wet, and runny.
Some pictures turn out pretty nice,
and some look pretty funny.

Soon it's time to exercise.
So they head out for the gym,
where some learn how to kick a ball,
and others learn to swim.

When dinosaurs get hungry,
it must be time for lunch.
Today it's prickly pizza,
their favorite thing to munch!

The recess bell begins to ring.
It's time to play outside.
They all take turns at hopscotch,
and ride the dino-slide.

Then come music lessons.
They learn a brand new song.

The music teacher swings a stick,
and taps his foot along.

Next, they learn their numbers,
and they learn how flowers grow.
But now the school day's over,
and it's time for them to go.

Dinosaurs all say goodbye,
and soon they're on their way.
But they'll be back tomorrow,
for another fun-filled day!